AF595990

TITLE

THE SCARLET TOWER

AUTHOR

FARHAN ILYAS

Chapter 1

"Center your psyche. Allow all that to leave it." I say in a quiet voice as Odelia shut her eyes. We were on the floor of the cellar. It was the most secure spot to rehearse, long periods of charms encompassed us forestalling supernatural over-burden and any wanderer enchantment from leaving the concrete around us. Additionally, nothing would get harmed since it was a vacant room.

"Presently to you consider your powers and what keeps them down. Presently let it go, envision it vanishing.

You have no sentiments. You are a conductor for your powers, allow them to free." I say. Her face was aloof, which was a decent sign. We had been going this for quite a long time. Control of our powers was perhaps of the main thing.

Alongside doing what we must to make due. I grinned as water topped off with lower part of the storm cellar. I gave her more guidelines about how to manage the water. Till she was excessively worn out to do much else.

We generally needed to prepare until somebody imploded, the way it must be. I sent her higher up yet didn't follow yet, I watched the water gradually empty out through the floor. I took a full breath this was getting increasingly hard. I was getting to delicate, something I can't bear to have occur. It was excessively risky. The chuckling from

higher up was decent excessively pleasant. I was too used to things being ordinary, and nothing could be typical. It seemed like the battle was leaving me which was awful. I expected to keep my edge, yet I was so drained, burnt out on doing this, burnt out on losing.

We would need to go soon, not on the grounds that they were totally prepared but since I was getting excessively appended.

She would be vexed assuming that I got to connected to them. They were fighters nothing else, that is the manner by which She said I should think about them. I moaned and went higher up I could do this.

Everybody was jabbering around the table eating I took my things and went higher up I saw Medusa watching me leave everybody. She was the first I found

at the point when I was making our little pack. We just every had a modest quantity of individuals simpler to prepare and control.

There are 5 young ladies this time. Medusa was one of the more uncommon ones I have at any point found, the ability to freeze time is nearly as uncommon as what I do. She will be satisfied.

Subsequent to eating and sitting arranging how we needed to help this I got up and pulled on my running shoes. We had just moved here; exploring was finished before we settled to ensure the region was protected. We could never have any of those beasts close to us. I went through my window so not to terrify anybody in the house it was dim and late.

Moving out of the curiously large tree-house we resided in was more troublesome than I previously expected. Which of all time Princeps, Latin in a real sense meaning pioneer we are so imaginative, chose making a tree-house as a protected house needed to have fight shock or something to that effect.

Truly it was fun yet so illogical.

Running caused me to feel far improved about everything, since nothing is more regrettable or better than running. The consume in your lungs the battle with your brain and knowing the way that your legs could convey you for eternity. I ran past where we had explored into another piece of the timberland.

My psyche meandered and that is the very thing I fault for not seeing it immediately.

I recalled being more youthful a little 10-year-old going through the timberland with her running close to me letting me know I needed to run quicker run better. She was preparing me something we as a whole required. She prepared harder than I do.

My foot found something sending me to the floor. I moved coming up into a hunker on protection. I saw what stumbled me it was only a tree root. I murmured and stood up then, at that point, heard a snarl.

"Who are you?" A voice inquired. I froze I knew what a snarl implied. This was terrible.

Rather than a response I dodged and swung around my leg raised for a round house kick and got the

beast in the stomach rattling him for a few moments. Barely enough time for me to turn and run through the forest. I didn't return to the house. I couldn't bring that beast back home and hazard the young ladies getting injured, or more regrettable not understanding what must be done. I heard more strides, extraordinary, the beasts were set up in packs very much like us. Thus, the one I kicked called to a greater amount of those things, doubtlessly more visitor monitors.

They didn't call the Alpha for something little as a

'human' intruder. They were wildly regional. Which was sad for my moron self, I ran straightforwardly

into their domain. I went through a stream, trusting it would jumble my aroma and afterward into town wheezing delicately. I listened near ensure I lost them previously strolling through town. We had gotten comfortable an external town of Boise, Idaho. Ought to have realized that Idaho would have wolves.

I returned to the house that was not exactly in the town since well it was a tree house that would appear strange to ordinary individuals. We didn't come into town frequently. The young ladies went to class at the neighborhood government funded school.

I fortunately had moved on from the damnation of secondary school last year. I remained at home and dealt with the house and kept us safe. I successfully returned into my room and set down gazing at the roof. We were unable to remain long. However, the young ladies

weren't prepared and there was just a single additional spot to go… seven days, in the event that I could allow them seven days then I could get the all set to the red pinnacle. With my choice made I nodded off trusting I didn't simply condemn us to Demise.

I was worried about how close the bunch of beasts was. How did we not notice this, I felt like I might have fizzled. However long they didn't find us, we would be alright.

On the off chance that they did, we would be compelled to battle before we were prepared. I realized I could proceed to kill them all. Yet, the more extended I was away from Her the more I would have rather not battled them. The more I didn't feel they were the adversary. I concluded I needed to figure out additional about them and in the event that we expected to leave at the present time. I overlooked the prospect that no matter what I did they would kick the bucket. Like all of the others.

I left early afternoon when the young ladies were all at school. I strolled through the forest gradually focusing, for some reason we could continuously tell where new domains were, we additionally had better than expected smell and could move quicker. We had more strength also everything connected with the beasts to us that we needed to keep firmly

locked away. Meandering around I recollected when I did that for many years. Just meandered after it occurred. It was while meandering that I viewed as Her. Which saved me. I tracked down near the edge of their

domain and moved up a tree and watched the

Chapter 2

visitor monitors. They should be an enormous pack for having so many gatekeepers. I saw or smelled no scouts

meaning they couldn't have cared less about the people or anything near them we might be protected. I escaped the tree gradually. When on the ground I heard a watchman yell, poop how could they notice me. They were excessively near run away. Along these lines, I turned and went after them. We battled for seconds when he figured out how to hit sufficiently, I felt my wrist snap. Eventually I had gone to where my back was to their domain. A dumb move. I would have continued to battle however the most lovely aroma entered my nose. It resembled new bread and the ground soon after downpour. I smothered the hazardous side and a snarl and gone to stir things up around town smelling beast who had figured out how to come up behind me. Yet, the beast detected that and snatched my arm. He stuck me against a tree. Squeezed against the tree his sparkling wolf eyes sparkling in to mine he expressed the word, what showed we needed to leave very soon.

"Mate." he says seeming as though he just viewed as the best treasure on the planet. He didn't appear to understand that he had recently tracked down the deadliest toxin. The mixing

in my chest was risky. In this way, I drove him away overlooking the agony of my messed up wrist.

"Try not to contact me." I say letting the power and power I had spill through my voice, She said it was from my birth I was a conceived pioneer. I saw his little wolf companion bow his head. I felt a savage fulfillment that I made him agreeable yet the kid before me appeared

unaffected. In this way, he was an alpha, the most horrendously terrible of the sort.

The ones who must be annihilated the most. I pushed down not just the presence coming into my brain and looked at him without flinching. An immediate test however he wasn't focusing he was seeing me befuddled.

Most likely in light of the fact that he however he felt something in me, something calling to him. I felt that dreadful beast in me pushing against my jail I made for it. I pushed it away I expected to move away. I feigned exacerbation and strolled away I realized he wouldn't follow. I strained my shoulders overlooking the crying from him, that was reverberated in the dim pieces of my psyche. The parts that I had some time in the past spurned, the parts that needed to annihilate me.

I returned home and attempted to fail to remember his astounding voice and how great he looked. I cleaned the house and requested take out for the young ladies. I prepared with our most youthful Veronika, she was like 14 and had some control over fire. She was generally so quite sweet.

Preparing her made me grin since she was silly, she did every last bit of her powers like an anime character she made me watch it once. I don't recall what she called it yet, it was enjoyable. I simply lacked the capacity to deal with fun.

Subsequent to preparing her it helped me have an improved outlook on him.

Made his face blur from my psyche, yet more awful about what I was getting them in to, that they were never ready for the revulsions that going to her would cause them..

They snarled snatching me and yanking me along overlooking my arguing and crying. I was tossed down on the ground before them the board. They checked out me briskly.

"Send her to Spain with the other disgusting witches."

They say the men get me once more and brutally hauled me outside. The sun dazed me I had been locked away for seven days in a dim cell that smelled of pee and unwashed bodies. I was pushed on to the unpleasant floor some truck with bars. As we drove werewolves and people spit and hassled me. They didn't have the foggiest idea about my wrongdoing however realize that I had effectively enraged the gathering. At long last, at the line of Spain I was tossed out of the truck. They beat me, my shouts becoming whines as they left me for dead right over the boundary. I nestled into held back to pass on. I needed to bite the dust.

I awakened gasping and canvassed in sweat from my bad dream it was actually a memory. A memory for a long time back, however something I was unable to neglect. For that reason I realized she was right; they were beasts and must be eliminated for the endurance of our species.

The following morning, I was hysterical. The bad dream cracked me out such a lot of I was unable to rest not on the grounds that it was unnerving, and the beasts lived near us. It generally cracked me out so that wasn't a component, something about it generally felt bogus like somebody had gotten into my mind and changed things. However, I didn't know anybody who could do that. I realize that telepaths could, if they were adequately strong, change recollections. I had never been around telepathic however, so they had to be genuine.

After the young ladies went to class I pondered my next move. There is still parts to do. I needed to sort out the quickest and most secure method for getting into the pinnacle. Everything would be alright once we got to the pinnacle.

I chose to make some more espresso then check delineates. I enjoyed maps more than telephones something about having it truly in her grasp. I looked we needed to get from Idaho to Colorado. A more drawn out drive however with so many of us ready to drive we could turn off before we got as well tired.

Subsequent to arranging our direction, I murmured I had nothing I could truly do right now. They young ladies didn't know we were leaving at this point. I didn't have the foggiest idea how to break it to them.

Since they had hardly any familiarity with it, I couldn't simply begin pressing.

I never snoozed well so all things being equal I just sat outside thinking as I taste my espresso. I recollected the initial time I at any point had espresso. I shut my eyes and thought internal like I had been educated to recall obviously recollections and let myself hit home to the memory.

I was freezing I had been meandering around for a long time searching for anyplace to be. I was in Spain. Where I had been

The memory went fluffy and the words cruelly rang out in my mind, "Expelled, exiled and tossed out like junk beaten and left to kick the bucket by the beasts of the werewolf gathering" The memory returned to center.

It was a freezing and pouring. I gazed upward when I saw pleasant boots remaining before me. Like extremely pleasant boots, they were croc boots with a little heel to them. A wonderful woman remained before me holding her umbrella over me. Which was unique, very few individuals would help a teen looking vagrant around here. Since well teens around here preferred to take.

"You appear to be cold sweet thing. Here drink this it will help."

She said offering me the cup. I took it and took a taste. It was warm and sort of unpleasant with a touch of sweet like milk. I saw her trusting she would let me know what the screw I was drinking.

"Its espresso minimal one. The gathering sent you, here didn't they. I can help you. Accompany me. There is a gathering of us. We have a pinnacle called the Violet pinnacle. I chose she is protected, something in my mind said that she could never hurt me. I opposed that idea briefly

prior to gesturing and going with her. A tad; I set aside some margin to concentrate on her. She was in a decent lengthy channel coat; under was decent fabrics. It seemed to be a pantsuit or some likeness thereof. Her boots I understood were repulsing water.

Indeed, even after she ventured the ground sullen dry for a couple seconds. She was semi tall, with earthy colored hair in delicate twists.

Her face looked more cut off like those films with the cut off overseer for a halfway house.

We came to the pinnacle, it was a wonderful radiant violet variety in the open country. It shone like

gems, the grounds were gigantic. Other than individuals in general, there was lovely plants all over. I appreciated perusing furthermore, there was such countless wonderful spots to sit and peruse.

This seemed to be the best spot of all time.

I panted checking out at everything. It wasn't pouring any longer, there was individuals overall around outside. Every one of them rehearsing

sorcery. I was glad and stunned. Individuals could simply do wizardry uninhibitedly here! I realize that I was unable to do that, I was perilous the committee said so and to that end they sent me to the pinnacles.

They exiled you and left you for dead.

The idea came into my head and I wrinkled my

eyebrows, what? That isn't what occurred. They brought me to the furthest extent that they would be able, I just got lost. I turned upward when

one of the older folks came up and removed the woman unobtrusively chiding her about something. Strange. Someone else came and showed me around. She got me a difference in fabrics and was exceptionally great. She had a British inflection.

I was told about how the violet pinnacle was a preparation place for those of our sort. To assist us with becoming valuable and ready to control our powers.

I moaned delivering myself once again from the memory, that was a great time. I was in the violet pinnacle for quite a while, with her. Then, at that point, when misfortune struck the pinnacle we left together, and she carried me to the red pinnacle. At some point just after the misfortune something changed in her. Something made her scornful towards whatever wasn't our sort. I was unable to pinpoint the specific time, however it seemed like once she got disdain full it was difficult to clash with her at all when around her. I recall that I proved unable indeed, even think a conflict. However, that could simply be my

memory issues. It was difficult to recollect a ton of things any longer. I was unable to recollect where I was before the gathering tossed me out and passed on me to kick the bucket. Then after that the recollections come in streaks and once in a while try not to remain. I ambiguously feel like I found it once in the red pinnacle's library, however I don't recall what it was. I in all actuality do recollect it was in some kind of spell book. I additionally recall conversing with her about it and something occurred. Then, at that point, the library was mystically locked, and I couldn't go in any longer. She said that something perilous was in there that we were unable to manage our selves.

The abnormal thing about the red pinnacle was simply no one was there when we arrived. Like they were all gone, however as of late there wasn't any residue, and it wasn't from cleaning spells since there wasn't any on there.

She let me know it was on the grounds that the beasts unexpectedly and severely went after and killed every one of them with out caution. It should be valid in any case were, right? However something generally messed with me about that, there was no bodies couldn't we track down bodies or blood or something like that? I murmured once more and got up I expected to get back. I generally realized I had been away for a really long time when I began to question things. Everything would be better once we got to the pinnacle.

I was perched on the patio partaking in the outside. The trees influenced delicately in the light breeze. I genuinely trust we live in the most lovely spot, yet I was unable to be taken too severely I had never left the pack grounds but to go to the nearby human town. I tasted my espresso watching I had about an hour prior to preparing. I prepared with a gathering of folks that were my age in the pack, we prepared a few times each day. It was for security since we had heard bits of gossip about mysterious creatures going after more modest packs. We were a more modest pack. We had a few silly names we called our gathering none of which are at any point stood up of our gathering. Since I am the alpha's child, and the future alpha doesn't mean I wouldn't be constantly prodded by everybody. We were all like family here since we were so little.

I murmured taking a gander at the sky making me consider my mate's blue eyes. She was the most astounding young lady I had at any point had the joy of checking out. I really wanted to however, feel a touch miserable. She ran from me. I had consistently longed for a mate. Somebody who might comprehend me best, somebody to cherish me. We didn't date beyond mates. What while the contention could be made that it hurt our social turn of events, we were little and customary. In this way, we didn't date anybody yet our mate.

What befuddled me and my wolf the most was she

smelled practically like a human, yet there was a bizarre thing with that smell. It made me consider the widows

who lost their significant other and their wolf passes on to keep the human side from going crazy. I had to know more about who and what she was. I got up murmuring and extending. I took my espresso with me inside to find one of my pack individuals, and an old buddy.

I went to his room and thumped prior to opening the entryway. I was gotten with heaps together to the roof of books.

They went generally around the room his bed was a sleeping cushion on top of books. He was sitting in a corner his nose in, you got it, a book.

"Fella, come on this is going crazy you know we have a colossal pack library you can keep these in." I say snickering a little. Roman just shrugged at me.

"I really want them close for research." He said he was our principal legend/anything in a book, individual. You expected to know anything you asked Roman. He was an immense resource for our pack. I shook my head at him and went along with him on the ground.

"I really want to know something." I say which he recently gestured giving me the look that this was clear since I came to his room and sat. Rather than simply hauling him out in the sun like I regularly did.

"There is a bunch of young ladies close to us. Furthermore, I mean just young ladies.

Chapter 3

They smell human yet just to a point." I say and he checked me out.

"I'm great yes. However, I am not a supernatural occurrence specialist! For poops purpose. I want far more data." He said shaking his head at me.

"Accompany me then, at that point. We will go covert agent." I proposed. He wavered then gestured. I mind connected my father that Roman and I planned to go out for a run. I couldn't let him know we truly doing. I had a premonition that he wouldn't support.

We left the region and I began sort of meandering around.

"You don't have the foggiest idea where their pack is isn't that right?" Roman asked and I gave him a timid grin.

It required about thirty minutes to track down their place. By that time, it was as am 7, each of the young ladies had knapsacks on what's more, were strolling to a vehicle. Thus, they go to class, a couple of the pack individuals go to class. Perhaps I could ask them to watch out for them to attempt to discover something furthermore, obviously ensure they are protected.

I had a doubt, or perhaps it was an expectation, that they were simply making tracks from somebody. On the off chance that they

were then it very well may resemble those heartfelt motion pictures that the young ladies in the pack were continuously watching, where the fellow saves the young lady.

Roman was watching different young ladies while I was looking for my little mate. Where was she I could feel she was some place close. When the young ladies left, we snuck nearer to the tree house they resided in. Not going to lie it was epic.

I moved up to through a window Roman behind me.

We wound up in a room that was blue with water and fish things all over. It looked cool however very prohibitive, practically like which ever young lady lived here could just consider water. I saw every little thing about it was simple tidy up. Like in the event that they expected to abruptly leave then, at that point, they could. Strange. We investigated the house in the long run separating.

I was by a window watching my mate. I had seen as her; she was similarly just about as lovely as whenever I first saw her. I realize that I was so far gone for her, yet she was my mate, so it was alright. She was sitting with her back to me watching out at the yard. In any case, something felt like she wasn't actually there, similar to she was somewhere within her mind.

I watched her till Roman came to me he looked among me and the young lady. Prior to hauling me away.

When we were far enough away, he halted me.

"That young lady in there is your mate, isn't she?" He asked a bless his face. I really wanted to grin back and gesture.

"No doubt she is my mate. Along these lines, discover much else about them?" I asked ideally. Roman's grin broke down.

"Not yet, I want additional time. Why haven't you told your father?"

I just shook my head.

"I know it's moronic, yet I might want to prevail upon her first, before I tell my father and he gets her to the pack."

Roman just gestured his getting it. We strolled back what's more, I went to prepare while he went to attempt to find out about my mate.

I told Annika not to go to class today. I really wanted her to accompany me some place. She thought about what it was, she was the second young lady I found. She then assisted me with selecting the rest. I should enlighten her regarding how great of a princeps Annika would be, yet something about having her know, genuinely understand what I was doing made me reluctant. I was going delicate, I should have been around her. She had a way about her, a method for causing all that to appear like we had to the entirety of this poop. Practically like she could change considerations yet that was insane, she wouldn't do that. I had known her for just about 20 years now, so why would she lie to me.

Before she saved me, I was in Spain for a period however what occurred there is fluffy. All I can genuinely recall of my past is that bad dream, now and again unusual unexpected glimmers of recollections and afterward her tracking down me. The recollections appear to constantly begin returning the more I am away from the pinnacle. Showing I needed to get back before long, it was clear I would have rather not recalled those recollections.

It was toward the middle of the afternoon when Annika and I went out furthermore, strolled for quite a while. We strolled peacefully, my past hanging weighty at the forefront of my thoughts, what Annika was pondering I couldn't really understand.

We arrived at some train tracks and followed them. The reason we were out now was that I had detected that some young lady with new powers was somewhere near here. I carried Annika because of her capacity to detect and change feelings. Young ladies who had quite recently tracked down their abilities can be extremely hazardous as well as probably self-destructive. I was mindful so as to hold my feelings back behind a thick wall, in the event that Annika could feel my fear, responsibility, and pity she would address me. I was unable to let that happen we had an excess of that must be finished.

Everything would be okay once we got to the pinnacle, something I needed to hush up about rehashing.

We both saw the young lady sitting on the edge of the tracks.

Annika gave me a look which implied she was feeling severely, which was clear she was crying delicately and seemed as though she was considering leaping off the extension.

She was something youthful likely around 13 or thereabouts. I could tell that she was one of us, yet I was unable to determine what type she was since her powers were so immature. We approached her and sat on one or the other side of her. She looked into surprised and a touch protective. Once more, not a shock, I had been informed I was threatening, I my long red hair was maneuvered once more into a braid and I was in jean shorts and a tank top appearance of how fit I was. I prepared frequently, Annika then again was wonderful with light hair and green eyes, yet something about her was consistently a touch disrupting. Like a specialist who continuously knew the most horrendously awful things about you. Being the princeps I talked first.

"Howdy, let me suppose you have been an outsider since you have abilities" I say getting directly to the point she gestured. I grinned at her pleasantly. The youthful ones were the least demanding to have join. They didn't have the foggiest idea instructions to deal with themselves, the more seasoned ones who had had the option to endure required really persuading.

"How about you accompany us then? We give homes to the individuals who don't have one since they are strong like you." Annika says the young lady thinks to and fro

Chapter 4

between us then gestures. Her eyes would in general wait a little too lengthy on me. A piece of it might have been on the grounds that she could feel my power. The more awful choice was that she could perceive something was off with me. The young lady concurred furthermore, strolled with us. Something about the way she so immediately concurred with us had me a touch dubious. It was excessively simple.

I constrained myself to disregard my questions and consider how she would be satisfied to such an extent that another was found.

Annika gave her a tissue to clean her face and accompanied her to the house for testing. We just had a couple of something else days until we would leave however she may as yet be valuable contingent upon her powers.

In the wake of acquainting her with everybody and giving her some food, I took her to the cellar. Testing was straightforward we sat in the preparation room and followed a few activities. I had her sit on the mat and shut her eyes. I asked her to envision a wall among her and all the other things. That was overwhelmingly significant, besides the fact that it forestalls any undesirable consideration from other people who are not on our side. Yet, it additionally kept that risky thing toward the rear of our psyches hindered. Which was the reason it was terrible to such an extent that It

was getting through the wall as a result of that kid, it would annihilate you on the off chance that you let it. That is the principal thing she

educated me.

After a wall I asked to her become settled and tell me what she looked about her. She sat briefly thinking then talked.

"you are thinking about what kind of abilities I have. You additionally are considering heading to the red pinnacle not flying and there is a kid with green eyes however then, at that point, it is all fluffy." She said her eyebrows wrinkled in focus. I felt my heart stop.

"How was that?" she asked grinning, I faked a grin and tapped her head.

"Awesome. Presently don't educate anybody concerning your power yet okay?" I asked and she gestured and went higher up. She looked back, something in her look caused me to feel like I had quite recently been played. I shook my head it was simply me being jumpy.

I went to my room and plunked down. I thought holding a little mirror and reached her. She replied after a few moments her picture grinning back at me. She had delicate silver hair and a harsh face, yet she grinned marginally when she saw me. Her grin never contacted her eyes.

"Arlie. Great to see you alive. When are you coming home?" she asked consistently business, I had been away

from home for around 3 years finding, more like gathering the young ladies. Gathering them and acquire them to a repulsiveness filled world, some portion of me felt that it would be better in the event that I never tracked down them. I overlooked that I simply required to return to the pinnacle.

"In three days so on Sunday." I say and she gestured and made a note some place.

"The number of young ladies that have you found?" She asked this was the subject I needed to converse with her about

"I have 6 with me now." I say and she grinned broadly

"A decent sum, you have acquired one since we last talked." She said looking satisfied, she was going to not be satisfied.

"Indeed, she is youthful we found her a couple of days prior. She was feeling untouchable and discussing self destruction. We saved her." I let's assume she gestured yet didn't appear to be keen on my words.

She was recording something, probably fight

plans. I generally felt as she didn't mind the number of young ladies passed on she just thought often about the number of beasts kicked the bucket. In any case

there was dependably setbacks in war.

"What is her power?" she asked, this was the terrible part. I intellectually pre-arranged myself to be hollered at. She saw I didn't answer immediately and gazed upward gazing at me through the mirror, she wouldn't ask two times.

"She is telepathic, more remarkable than I have ever go over previously." I say she looked very disturbed furthermore, furious.

"You have not dealt with her? For what reason did you not send her away? She is risky, and you are imperiling all that we have worked for." She said her voice was not raised yet it actually made me shudder marginally and be cheerful I was in one more state from her. She was perilous like this.

"She is a kid and would bite the dust all alone." I say she glared more diligently

"She wants to kick the bucket. You have gotten delicate. We will talk a greater amount of this when you arrive, and don't even think about it carry that vial animal to the pinnacle. She should be killed." She requested and disengaged the mirror from her own. I moaned and wanted to cry. I was delicate, excessively delicate.

I put down the mirror. That went comparably well as I figured it would. I could hear the young ladies snickering first floor. That sounded excessively pleasant, I needed to return to the red pinnacle. When I did all future great once more. Assuming that it was at any point alright in the first place.

I heard a thump on my window. I investigated and saw the idiotic alpha. I didn't have the energy to battle with him. The day was depleting as it was, and afterward with the felt that every one of the young ladies snickering down there their

blood is on my hand. Thus, I did nothing when he opened the window and ventured into my room. He looked so great, however I realized where it counts he would continuously look great to me. His green shirt upgraded those green eyes. He was in ball shorts flaunting tan pleasantly ripped legs. I ought to quit looking at him. I made due to pull my eyes away as he drew nearer.

He sat on my bed exceptionally near me. Our legs contacting just so marginally. The contact made it hard to plainly think also, made me gaze toward his face. The baffled look all over illuminating effectively the thing he was thinking. He needed to understand what I was, also he proved unable comprehend the reason why I wasn't feel as he was. Yet, I was feeling that attract to allow him to hold me and kiss me. To tell him all that and have his assistance. I wanted assistance.

Something was the matter with my head. In any case, I proved unable. He was the adversary, right?

"You ought to go." I say delicately. I don't recall when I wound up resting up against his shoulder his arm around me. He felt so overall quite warm. He likewise smelled astonishing.

I inclined away and he moaned getting up. He was regarding my desires… Are each of the beasts like him so amenable? I felt so confounded, the Scarlet pinnacle. The pinnacle what's more, her were the main constants the main things I could trust. I was unable to trust the young ladies or the delightful beast

before me, I was unable to try and trust my own psyche.

Chapter 5

"For what reason do you drive me away?" He asked remaining in front of me presently so close his sent filling my nose. His moving endlessly and his astounding smell made a mixing in the haziest profundities of my brain. It was an admonition I required him to leave now, before It reached out. I knew I needed to come clean, I needed to hurt him only a bit of spot, so I don't end of killing him.

"Since I will annihilate you. I will break you as it were you love then leave you where nobody can fix you. I will be what you love then I will compel you to look as you see it change into an ugly beast. You are way excessively great for me. In the event that I see you once more, I will kill you." I say

furthermore, push him through my window. I shut it rapidly and lit candle to dispose of the sent. I needed to keep It under control, it had been for such a long time since It had attempted to return. In any case, I wouldn't let It, I would feel an excess of agony. It would obliterate me, annihilate us. I had assembled so a lot; I had been alive for north of 400 years and I wouldn't allow everything to go to squander. It wasn't simple keeping myself alive for such a long time I needed to do numerous things that were not by any stretch of the imagination moral. I

wouldn't rest till every one of them were dead. They were the foe something I would always remember. They need us dead.

I stopped; how could I realize I was alive for a very long time. I hadn't been alive for that long. Just like 50, we age more slow than people, making more like a 20-year-old. I wasn't alive for that long. What's more, I don't recollect a large portion of my life how do I have at least some idea that I did corrupt things. My head hurt so awful like two things were battling in my mind. Like two lives were attempting to dominate.

I felt something wet on my hand and thoroughly searched in an ordinary mirror and saw I was crying. I don't recollect the last time I cried. I moaned I expected to follow through with something. I stuffed a little sack and afterward left through the window.

I strolled for quite a while, until I got into the city. I looked around at the night life, every one of the people processing around carrying on with their lives. I needed to take off, to begin once again. I could do it; I had a greater number of abilities than killing beasts. I sat in a recreation area it was dim and I was separated from everyone else. For what reason would I be able to

simply be let be.

I knew why, since I had something important to take care of. The world would never go back assuming that those beasts are permitted to be even close to us. They will kill us first then they will continue on and kill the people in general. That is everything she said me. I could trust her. It was time now, I needed to tell the

young ladies.

I returned home the young ladies were still up watching a film. I came in and they generally grinned.

"We need to talk. Meet me in the storm cellar." I say and return down the stepping stool. I strolled to the secret entrance that lead to the storm cellar. I could hear the young ladies following me. They generally sat on the floor. Casandra, the clairvoyant sat looking befuddled. The other young ladies didn't look befuddled, simply prepared. They could all detect I was getting anxious and likely expected that I planned to tell Once more, them we are moving.

"I have numerous things to tell you. To begin with, we are leaving in three days. This move anyway isn't similar to the others. We are going to the red pinnacle. I haven't enlightened you up to this point since you were not prepared, you are currently. We are at war." I say I see stunned faces all over. I take a full breath prior to proceeding, the young ladies are great prepared fighters. They won't hinder me.

"There are beasts that are attempting to kill us. They chase us for game and kill us. They are part wolf and can change into wolves. The red pinnacle is the most secure spot as far as we might be concerned, however the beasts are familiar it. We needed to keep

moving as I prepared you, so we wouldn't be found. There is a woman she is the top of the red pinnacle. She knows instructions to dispose of the beasts. The red pinnacle is the

final pinnacle of our sort. Quite some time ago there used to be more, yet the beasts have been obliterating them." I express stopping briefly I see Casandra looked much more stunned and furthermore extremely stressed. She ought to be, on the off chance that we didn't kill the beasts first, we would all bite the dust.

"They are really beasts. They kill honest people. I have seen them butcher little youngsters for simply being there."

I say and Casandra looks befuddled, that is peculiar. I overlook it for the present.

"Now that you know what is happening and know why I have prepared you so hard. We need to pack. The following couple of days proceed with like you have been previously. At the point when you return from school, I maintain that all of you should pack and afterward we will train. When we arrive at the red pinnacle we might be under assault all of a sudden. I maintain that all of you should be ready." I say and pass on them to talk about among themselves. I tapped on Casandra's shoulder and gestured for her to follow me.

"I realize we just tracked down you, so I figure you ought to go. If you go south, you ought to have the option to track down another gathering of individuals. Like us who can prepare you better before you need to manage this bad dream." I say. I had my brain protected, serious areas of strength for however she seemed to be, she wasn't educated

the most effective method to peruse safeguards. The fact that I makes it crucial

kept it safeguarded in light of the fact that south wasn't a greater amount of us.

South

was where the beast pack was. She would bite the dust there, I done whatever it takes not to ponder how I was sending her to demise. Very much like the wide range of various young ladies I was taking to the red pinnacle. I murmured delicately and she checked me out.

"You realize you are sending them to their demises. She truly destroyed you. You truly accept they are beasts, even with a mate. How could she get so many misleading recollections to you?" Cassandra said delicately. I checked her out.

"Excuse me?" I say overreacting, who is this young lady? She can't have known all of this, what does she mean misleading recollections? Then she contacted my head, and everything went dim.

This was by a long shot the most terrible task I had at any point been on. I realize that it was awful when I was given the task. The document was extremely uncovered which was rarely a great sign. The record recently expressed that there was doubt of one of our sort going rouge and acquiring individuals to satisfy an individual feud. I currently realized it wasn't Arlie. It was whoever ran the pinnacle, a pinnacle that didn't exist. At least as per the board.

I realize I looked exceptionally youthful, that was with the assistance of one of the illusionists from the Gray pinnacle. I was about as old as Arlie. The record referenced that it was

just youthful of our sort who were gathered. The way the battled was unnerving.

Chapter 6

I realized she felt regretful about it, I could effortlessly read that to her. Her safeguards areas of strength for were yet, in an unusual way they had secondary passages for individuals who were telepaths to enter her internal most brain.

Much more terrible she had attempted to dispose of me and I needed to take her out and take out that memory. Which is the way I perceived how terrible her psyche was, somebody had screwed up some poo in there. It was a wreck and I was unable to see anything about her passed aside from some abnormal wrecked recollections. Somebody had been altering with her brain for a really long time.

I had figured out how to move away for a couple of hours. This was terrible so awful. I dove deep into the forest. Going north, since I have no faith in going south. Particularly after Arlie proposed I go South and had the idea in her psyche that I would kick the bucket assuming I went that way.

I sat up in a tree to stowed away and quieted myself. I was a damn great telepath yet coming to the nation over was troublesome and would require the entirety of my fixation. I overlooked everything, as my preparation showed me, and

reached my manager.

I heard her voice a touch static like briefly previously it cleared.

"Cassandra, I am happy to hear from you. Have you made contact?" He asked, Morpheus was the most grounded mind peruser we had, and was my contact for this mission.

Because of its significance he was at that point with the committee prepared to give any updates that we essential. I murmured, considering how to say this.

"I have, Morpheus it is such a lot of more regrettable than we first envisioned. Whoever is driving this entire situation has all the control. They have plotted the princeps that werewolves are a definitive foe. The princeps' name is Arlie. I have close to zero familiarity with her. What I have so far is that she is around 50 years of age, she was in Spain for some time. She has had tower preparing yet the recollections around that and her winding up in Spain are broken." I say giving Arlie's data first. Morpheus was a tad. I realized he was providing requests to look records for her, as well as telling the gathering her name in the event that they definitely knew something about her.

"Okay we are looking now to check whether we can see as her. Is it as terrible as what occurred in Arizona?" He inquired.

In Arizona there a rebel bunch who needed to

open our reality to people and afterward be paid for

the people to be permitted to live. Which was awful and nearly caused a subsequent Salem witch preliminaries.

"It is much more terrible than Arizona. The head of the pinnacle has Arlie accepting that she has seen wolves commit terrible demonstrations, and that the red pinnacle is the as it were remaining pinnacle left. She accepts the wolves are driving us wiped out." I say scouring my head.

"Well poo. Any thoughts regarding their arrangements?" He asked I could see he was gnawing his fingernails. Awful thing to do if you ask me.

"They are anticipating leaving for a pinnacle in two days.

Some pinnacle called the red pinnacle, however I know all the towers there is no red pinnacle. Issue is I am not expected to go with them. She has proactively attempted to send me away. Mo she is intending to kill me. The head of the pinnacle told her I need to kick the bucket on account of my powers.

This is some powerful crap man, she has so many misleading recollections in her, that chief is quite a psyche peruser, and has been chipping away at her for quite a long time. When she begins to uncertainty what she is doing she returns to the pinnacle. Structure everything I can say when she is there that insidious individual wipes her memory and ensures she doesn't address." I say making a solid attempt not to bite my nails. The association we had right presently was giving me the very inclinations of propensities that he had, which could get

irritating. Or on the other hand extremely off-kilter if somebody appealing strolled by and you needed to lay down with them, then the other individual likewise felt that.

"OK we will be at the pinnacle in two days on the off chance that we would be able however

Cassy we don't have the foggiest idea where it is. You need to follow them some way or another. Along these lines, do you have any idea what Arlie's abilities

are?" Mo sounded stressed which was alarming he was regularly so quiet.

"No, she doesn't prepare with anybody and her recollections are impeded on it, yet this is an alternate block. She set up that block herself. Clearly, she honestly hate her powers. You should do explore on your end if she was ever with us previously. I stressed Mo. She feels strong without her utilizing any powers." I say. Mo doesn't answer for a brief period.

"Okay give your best and reach us when it protected to do as such. We will see what we can view as on her." He said and the association was broken. I influenced a piece in the trees.

That was depleting. I laid down for a little rest then, at that point, got down.

Time to see what was north of here that would kill me.

The walk was everlastingly and really horrendous, I am not a major devotee of a cardio.

At the point when I was at long last sufficiently north, I detected a pack. That seems OK she thinks they need to kill us. I was stowing away

out in a tree watching the pack when I saw the alpha's child. He very closely resembled the kid in her psyche. Thus, he is her mate. How can she block the mate bond so well that she isn't in steady distress?

I awakened with a dash of a migraine. I was in my room. Odd I don't recall coming into my room by any means last

night. Should be pressure, poop I have a lot to be worried about. I actually needed to get everybody together, cause it to appear as we were never there, and afterward move everybody to the tower securely. In conclusion battle in a conflict, a conflict that I proved unable help however feel we had no part in being in.

I got cerebral pains like this all the time at the pinnacle, so it was certainly not no joking matter I just overlooked it. It was just physical torment. I could disregard actual agony, she instructed me that so youthful. Said it was the best illustration anybody could instruct.

Shut out all of the aggravation then you couldn't have ever to feel it.

Now and then I felt like perhaps feeling torment could be a decent thing, wasn't it what should compel you understand that you want to stop what you are doing.

I at long last got up and glanced through the window. It was late in the day which implied the young ladies were at that point at the school, great I would have rather not mingled today. I didn't have any desire to see their confident face that I realize will be dead soon.

I kicked up and off pressing everything and gradually

bringing down the spells that were all around the house.

Chapter 7

We had a ton of spells develop from rehearsing as well as spells to keep us stowed away. Spells that make individuals abruptly need to head off to some place else when they get near the house. I felt terrible today, more awful than any time in recent memory prior to everything hurt. I could obstruct a portion of the aggravation in any case, not every last bit of it. No thought why everything hurt, except a little part

of me needed to see the alpha kid. I felt attracted to him. I concluded I was finished pressing for the day it was simply to discouraging.

I was extremely mindful that I was simply attempting to postpone the unavoidable, to slow down a conflict that was totally essential.

A conflict that could save our sort.

I wound up sitting toward the rear of the house watching the trees. I cherished the woods or used to something now about it repulsed me. I tasted my tea it was this dull tea that made me consider the time before Spain.

I was a diplomates little girl, in every case fashionable and well mannered. I was youthful and swinging on the swings. The swings here were so exceptionally fun, home didn't have swings like this. It was shady out and no other person was on the

jungle gym. Yet, that was alright, I jumped at the chance to play without anyone else

My feathery dress was a dazzling pink and I had coordinating shoes. It was essentially as beautiful as a princess dress. Father said we were hanging around for a significant gathering; it was generally an however, significant gathering. The best part was I would get to join the gathering. Father said the gathering was in support of me, they expected to see something. Which is extraordinary I generally have needed to assist my father with his work. Father can do cool supernatural stuff like the divine helpers in stories.

Mother came and got me from the swings. She ensured my dress was as yet decent prior to taking me in to the huge room where a lot of individuals in lengthy robes were. Mother let me know they were the board to our sort. They had me sit in a major seat and held my hands to check whether I had abilities.

They said it was too soon to determine what sort of abilities however that I rebelliously had abilities.

Father grinned and removed me to go play while mother conversed with the chamber.

I flickered and glanced around. That was an extremely old memory it was dig without a doubt, however I thought my folks passed on. Did they bite the dust later? For what reason wouldn't I be able to recollect

something as horrible as my folks own demises?

I felt cracked endlessly wild. My powers flexed

behind the walls I had fabricated. Fuck, I checked the grass out also, looked as the grass began kicking the bucket in enormous sums around me. I was hyper ventilating this was terrible I couldn't stop it.

"(name). breath follow my breaths. In 1, 2, 3 out 1, 2, 3."

Candace said she was before me. Where did she come from? She ought to in any case be in school. I followed her breathing and figured out how to quiet down and control my powers.

"What occurred?" she asked stressed I could tell she hadn't seen what I had done on the grounds that she didn't crack out at me.

"Nothing stressed over what could occur." I say delicately putting down. Candace sat close to me gnawing her lip she appeared to be so tangled.

"Have you at any point seen some other pinnacles?" She asked shifting her head.

"I was at the violet pinnacle before it was annihilated. However the red pinnacle is the sole survivor." I say feeling discouraged and depleted. All that actually harmed and that dull beast in my sub-conscience was needing to see the alpha kid. His eyes were tormenting me.

"At any point do you believe that the red pinnacle is deceiving you?" Candace said she was gazing directly ahead so I couldn't make heads or tails of her face.

"Indeed, however its simply me not having any desire to trust reality. It is a brutal and hard truth to acknowledge yet it is so. We are ceasing to exist since beasts like those wolves are killing us. They chase us for sport. The head of the pinnacle had her own family killed by those beasts she observed them butcher her kids. All she needed was harmony, in any case, they won't acknowledge that. They maintain that we should be totally cleared out." I say genuinely. Candace looked so miserable, it was a hard and unforgiving truth to swallow yet one needed to. You can not live with your head in the sand all of your life.

I concluded that Cassandra ought to go out together. We were leaving tomorrow, and I needed to sort out some way to ensure that she didn't accompany however didn't have any desire to hurt her. We were in a town a piece far away from our house. I didn't need Hunter tracking down us and Cassandra having the option to see excessively, I had gotten her far from all werewolves for good measure. Telepaths were all way as well thoughtful to those beasts and wrecked a greater amount of us.

As we strolled, I saw something. More like somebody that made my blood run cold. He had chaotic hair and dim sacks under his eyes. His garments made him look destitute, since it was worn out miss coordinated and loaded up with openings. His eyes contained ages of information; he was scouring his head. He had a journal and a pen

behind his ear. There was composing on his arms. He turned and met my look his eyes were recorded over as all prophets were. He knew what my identity was and what I would do, and that terrified me the most. I would have rather not heard how I planned to demolish these young ladies' lives. How I would get them generally killed for a purpose that wasn't initially mine. I was unable to hear that. Cassandra had seen him as well her eyes went wide and I snatched her arm hauling her away. She saw me befuddled.

"His psyche is so… " She followed off looking longingly back around the bend to where the prophet was. I had heard that a prophet mind was crazy loaded up with all the potential outcomes of what could be or what will be. So many choices, I would can't stand that, such countless various recollections that are not yours. I previously disliked

my brain I wanted nothing added to it.

"He is a prophet they are exceptionally perilous stay away from them." I say maneuvering her into the vehicle and driving home. That was excessively close prophets are hazardous since they know excessively and having Cassandra around him would subvert all that we have

worked for.

I had close to zero familiarity with prophets, they could be male or on the other hand female. Not at all like how for us we were all females, at least I don't recollect truly meeting a male that was of

our sort. Other than there are scarcely any of us now it didn't matter we were a withering race.

Chapter 8

However long that prophet didn't meddle, and Cassandra didn't peruse a lot all eventual great. We just needed to get to the pinnacle.

At the point when we returned home, I concluded it would have been a preparing day. I expected to feel like I was setting them up enough. Like they weren't simply grub in a conflict.

When a month we would go out to prepare in the forest we would all battle against one another once without powers also, once with powers. I realize I should do this consistently, yet they got so harmed without fail. I proved unable stomach it, so we just did it one time each month. Despite the fact that I realize it will simply hurt them all the more once we arrive.

In any case, some portion of me feels that they will all bite the dust regardless of how much we train. I shake my head to dispose of the horrible contemplations. I should have confidence.

We needed to go outside since the storm cellar wasn't large enough for this. This resembled a reenactment of what we were preparing for. To kill those wolves before they kill us. The young ladies currently realized that was what it was all going to pave the way to. The region was checked and found to be vacant. A border was set up so nobody would meander in unintentionally.

Then, at that point, we began we needed to initially battle with our powers since with powers it would be more perilous and afterward everybody would be excessively worn out to battle once more. Yet, we would battle a subsequent time, without powers everybody knew the stakes. I had everybody loosen up.

"You have thirty minutes, similar to ordinary sole survivor wins. Start." at the finish of my words disorder broke out quickly they were all on each other. Regularly when we prepared like this the champ didn't need to do dishes for a month. A decent award everybody felt.

Cassandra stood her ground since she could detect what they were contemplating doing straightaway, yet her absence of experience discharge she was out quick. The main standards were not to kill one another and when a bone is broken you are out. Cassandra got out by her leg being broken. I watched doing whatever it takes not to contemplate how assuming this was genuine how they would be destroyed. Cassandra sat at the lower part of the tree I was in watching. I didn't partake one since I didn't have to prepare with them since none of them were close to my level it wouldn't help me. Likewise, I can approach to handily kill them, my powers can never be utilized in a cordial battle.

Cassandra was watching me, not the battle. She looked extremely worried for me, no thought why. I realized I expected to figure out how to send her away. I would prefer not to need to kill her myself, I realized I wouldn't have the option to. I was excessively delicate. I expected to return to the pinnacle.

Odelia was the sole survivor for this one which was regular she was profoundly strong. A decent resource. Really I don't think she had done dishes since she appeared. Her water power's were hazardous once she learned she could make the water hot. Each of the young ladies with the exception of Medusa what's more, Cassandra had terrible water consumes.

"Thirty minutes get mended and invigorated and afterward you go once more." I say Gina our occupant specialist was occupied for the following couple of minutes recuperating everybody's wrecked bones.

The more troublesome one was on Medusa. Her arm bone was standing out of her skin which looked totally sickening. Notwithstanding, Medusa was generally excellent at mental things, so I had showed her a helpful little stunt. I educated her how to overlook torment. It was quite some time in the past I educated her that. Feels like a lifetime.

"So roman any thought what those young ladies are?" I ask taking note that Roman was beginning to get silver hair at 17 poor young men.

He murmured running his hand through his hair looking disappointed. I had asked him secretly to investigate the pack like gathering my mate ran.

"Nothing yet none of our books notice them. The human library could have something in an old legend what's more, legend book. They must be extremely old so might be the people have something however I can't ensure how precise it will be however." He says murmuring. I gesture giving him the consent, well as much authorization as I was permitted to give. I wasn't alpha yet, not until my mate acknowledged me and my father gave me the title. I chose to go assistance the unfortunate youngster, so I left with him.

We got to the library after around a 20-minute drive, had to take a vehicle it would be odd in the event that we just left the forest to the library. I expected to go for a run soon My wolf side was tingling to get out. Our wolves try not to have various characters or anything, they are a piece of us somewhat favoring the wild side. At whatever point we shift the wolf side is in charge, it can assume command in some cases, yet it doesn't have complex considerations. Just things like get food, get water, play, safeguard and of course be near our mates.

It required long stretches of sitting in the fantasies and legends segment. Which let me let you know not so much fun as one would

think, Roman had gone through the whole area

before he threw in the towel, so we left. As we left, we saw a few little kids stroll in one had brilliant pink hair. She looked at us and the other young lady with dark hair pulled her alone taking a gander at us dubiously.

They were a piece of my mate's pack. I needed to say something to them, yet the dark haired young lady seemed to be she could go after us.

Odd, they were behaving like we were a danger to them.

Significantly more interesting the young lady with pink hair watched me intently and seemed as though she needed to converse with me. They went inside the pink hair young lady being pulled alongside the other young lady. We moved into the vehicle and returned home.

My wolf could swear that they were wolves, however when he attempted to reach them nothing answered. They couldn't be wolves then, at that point; no werewolf didn't have a wolf.

I shook my head and zeroed in on driving back on to pack grounds. When there I escaped the vehicle extending, I honestly loved vehicle rides it was excessively confined. I was anticipating spending the remainder of my day unwinding perhaps going so that a run could check whether my mate was near.

Notwithstanding, the moment I began to stroll towards the woods another pack part came approaching me.

No thought who precisely it was, assuming that I glanced through the pack connect, I could figure out who it was nevertheless that was to such an extent work and they were by all accounts in a rush.

"Sir your dad wishes to see you promptly on dire pack business." They said I gestured and went to my dad's office, expressing farewell to a decent quieting evening. In this way, they were in a rush anything my dad

says to do implies everybody will rush to make it happen.

Chapter 9

I thumped on the thick wood entryway that lead to the alpha's office, and office that will before long be mine once I turn 21. I trust at that point my mate will permit herself to go along with me. I realize she really focuses on me however much I care for her. In the event that she doesn't then well, I can't become alpha without my Luna. I would have rather not needed to taken a picked mate it didn't appear to be as great truly.

I hear my dad's rough voice advising me to enter. The office is as one would expect, huge windows rule one side while shelves encompass the rest with a huge scaring work area sat at the focal point of the room.

Behind the work area my dad sat, he looked like a mountain, and appear to be nearly basically as old as one. He was arriving at his 50's with turning gray hair yet had a huge number of muscles. He gestured for me to sit in the seat inverse of him. In the wake of sitting he murmured, he looked tired, he had been alpha since his dad gave it to him at the point when he was 21. He appeared to be increasingly more drained later mother kicked the bucket a long time back. The main thing keeping him from going off the deep end was his affection for the pack.

"One of our partners was gone after." He said scouring his head, my eyes enlarged.

"Who? How might we help?" I asked and he grinned somewhat in pride. He generally said I was as able to help as he was as a young fellow. Which is the most noteworthy commendation I could get I simply needed to do right by him, that and have my mate.

"I need to send you with a few of your heroes, the ones that you have been preparing with. You will go to their guide. We are don't know what went after them. The as it were reports that we have is that somebody got into their pack also, seized the alphas youngsters. Whoever took them presently needs a conflict. A conflict we will give them. I need you to leave this evening." He said and I gestured my understanding.

Whenever I was excused, I went to track down my fighters. I cherished saying that.

I made sense of for them the circumstance and afterward to be prepared to leave this evening.

I needed to go visit my mate this evening to tell her farewell.

Something halted me however, I would see her once more.

Perhaps time with me away would assist her with understanding that we have a place together.

I gathered my pack and aided picked any additional weapons what's more, clinical supplies we would require. Then, at that point, when the opportunity arrived, we got into a vehicle to take us to a little air strip. Where we would take a little confidential plane to Colorado.

I needed to consider how to dispose of Candice. I escaped my room searching for her yet found she was gone with every last bit of her stuff. Great that was a positive thing, basically she presently got an opportunity to be liberated from our destiny. I realized I would at absolutely no point ever have the option to do this in the future; this was the last time I could at any point gather any troopers to battle this idiotic conflict.

Everything was gotten together now and in the vehicle. Actually I didn't cry or say anything only gestured for everybody to get into the huge SUV. I just permitted them to have a solitary bag of things. Only hence, so when we

expected to leave, we could immediately.

When all in the vehicle I began it and headed to the furthest limit of the carport. Then undeniably did a spell together and the house burst in the blazes. It consumed rapidly and afterward the fire finished leaving no hint of us. It was a decent otherworldly fire; we would have rather not been the reason for a huge fire or any such thing. We did in any case in our center consideration about nature, other than we are the ones who live here.

We took shifts on the drive, well we who are old enough to drive. It took some time, I demanded having music playing behind the scenes continually.

We drove up to a huge house the entryway was incredibly red, not dark like most would expect there was a broken house behind the entryway. I realized it was a deception.

I had everybody escape the vehicle with our stuff.

"Inner self effundet sanguinem de manibus inimicorum vestrorum ut defendat omnes" (I will spill out all the blood out of the hands of your foes, to shield) I say the heaviness of the words settle over me. There was no turning around now. The doors opened quietly; I heard the young ladies wheeze behind me the scene behind the doors had moved to an enormous monumental pinnacle. It gleamed in the light, all red. Taking a gander at it now it made me consider blood. It satisfied its name well, something felt off with it generally. I pushed ahead and we as a whole begun strolling towards what was my home for more than 300 years, I think. I genuinely am don't know any longer. The red tower. Eight crows took off of the pinnacle and over our head. The shudder ran down my spine as we strolled inside. Crows would in general carry forecasts with them, they were never great I felt. Eight crows meaning sorrow.

The pinnacle was similarly just about as amazing as it had consistently been, however the phony excellence had quite a while in the past worn off of me.

The young ladies were all murmuring delicately discussing how delightful it was. I had one earphone in as consistently since the airs method for jumbling your mine was with music. She had instructed me that, consistent music helped keep the beast back to me.

I saw Joan leave grinning at us as we strolled nearer.

She gave me a solid embrace, her grin never contacting her

eyes.

"I am so happy you made it here safe. Its so hazardous outside." She said and I saw all of the others gesturing with what she said.

"Presently we should get you inside and I will see what you have learned." We were driven inside. The overabundant magnificence of the spot could overpower. Within made you consider the more established Russian structures. It was astounding, I found myself unfit to zero in on the tile flooring. I gestured to Joan and left them with her. Part of me feeling like I was leaving them with a snake. My room was on the highest level. It didn't have anything in its dark walls without any hangings, white floor covering and white roofs.

The bed was dull oak with jail blue sheets. They were awkward yet nothing about the pinnacle was agreeable. I set down on the bed and let recollections stream over me.

"Once more. You should get this right." Joan requested, I attempted to battle her close by to hand battle once more. Once more, I bombed.

She was irate and snatched me she tossed me in one of the cells.

"You should figure out how to be better. In the event that you won't utilize your powers, then this is what you get." She hollered and left me there. I went through days in the cells. Such countless days.

I squinted returning to myself.

Chapter 10

I gazed up at the roof above me. It was white with a fan in the middle turning at a fast. The weight in my chest was killing me gradually. Filling my veins with the toxic substance of responsibility. The entryway opened I investigated at Joan she sat on the bed close to me. Her white hair contrasted the dim walls of my room.

"Try not to look so down now darling you have brought us great fighters. By and by you have done the red tower a help that will not before long be neglected. Will you remain this time or are you going to return out selecting?" She inquired. Briefly searching in her eyes I saw us how the wolves should see us, we were the genuine beasts. We tracked down pariah youngsters and took them made them warriors made them battle and kill for us.

Then, at that point, the second passed, it wasn't our issue that we had to battle to remain alive. It is the status quo and the way it will constantly be. Questioning our reasons made us frail, we must areas of strength for be that the beasts didn't kill us.

"I will remain till the snow passes." I say delicately she grinned also, tapped my knee then left me in the quietness of my room.

"There is not a glaringly obvious explanation to feel remorseful. You are simply guaranteeing

that your caring stays alive." I say prior to getting up. Like continuously I couldn't persuade myself that that was valid. I needed to perceive how my kin were fitting in to the pinnacle. However, regardless of my questions some way or another each time Joan conversed with be it seemed like she knew best, as I needed to pay attention to what she said. Her words generally wormed their direction in to my brain and caused me to do anything she desired. Pay attention to her generally, she should know best. Despite the fact that I was more seasoned than her by a long time, I think. I never asked you don't inquiry you do as she says and have a favored outlook on everything she says to you.

I moved every one of my things out around midnight before everybody awakened. I didn't have quite a bit obviously, I wasn't there for that long. They were leaving today, what's more, I expected to follow. Clearly Arlie wouldn't allow me to accompany, who at any point was in control clearly preclude it. Yet, the genuine inquiry was the reason? It couldn't be my age, there was that young lady who was more youthful than me. Perhaps it was my powers, I could see through the falsehoods that she held taking care of to her.

I thought about the number of others that were clairvoyant that had been shipped off bite the dust. How long had this been going on? I couldn't perceive I would have rather not jumped do profound into Arlie's mind on the off chance that I mess something up. It would be extremely awful

assuming I did that since alarm appears to make her powers go haywire.

Along these lines, I left and went into town, I had heaps of cash. There was a vehicle rental that I had seen when I went into the town with Arlie. I let the deception of my young age vanish and afterward found the knapsack I had reserved in a shrubbery along the street, I did that before they 'found' me.

In it was cash and my ID showing I was north of 21. Which I was I was 50 however looked around 21 so the ID was

reasonable.

I got an extremely normal exhausting vehicle. I didn't focus on what precisely with the exception of that it was a dark more modest vehicle. A sports vehicle would be too ostentatious, sad they were so significantly more amusing to drive. When I got the vehicle I went and stopped on an abandoned part by the house. They needed to take this street to leave by any means. Then I shut my eyes connecting for Morpheus.

We associated rapidly.

"Hi Cassy, what have you got?" He inquired

"I'm set to follow them once they leave. Arlie was in the violet pinnacle, however she thinks it got gone after and that any remaining pinnacles have been annihilated." I say then, at that point, stopping for him to depend the data to everybody else.

"Okay that is extraordinary data, ought to help the violet

tower doesn't take many individuals in by any stretch of the imagination. Other than its in

Spain, whatever else?" He inquired. He actually sounded stressed yet more confident today.

"Indeed, she has demise abilities Mo. Like serious demise powers, I tracked down her a piece prior overreacting the grass around her was kicking the bucket. On the off chance that I wasn't protected, she would

have killed me. She is so strong Mo. On the off chance that she starts to battle it will be a slaughter." I say. He was quiet for a long time.

"fuck. I need to go once you find the spot let us know furthermore, we will be there as quickly as time permits." He said and then cut the association this was terrible. Extremely terrible.

I took profound sluggish breaths and tasted my espresso. Then worked on putting spells on the vehicle so one I proved unable crash it. Second ones that would follow at a certain distance a vehicle. This would have been a long ride and with it following for me I might in any case rest and plan what to do.

It was around 10 am the point at which I saw the SUV emerge from the carport. I followed the vehicle and set the spell to keep me following them.

The vehicle halted before an entryway. I got out and snuck close everybody was watching the entryways as they opened.

Screw fuck, that was one unnerving pinnacle, it was in a real sense

dying. I followed inside then, at that point, concealed in the shrubberies. I have never been more joyful that I was extremely short, and that these shrubberies had no thistles. I looked as some more seasoned woman emerged from the pinnacle. I didn't perceive her by any means, so she wasn't one of the gatherings generally cared about.

She grinned at the gathering however appeared to be so phony. I could sense she was a really strong clairvoyant. She was the one who had been controlling Arlie.

I was unable to peruse anything on her. Her safeguards were strong and antiquated, similar to 500 years of age old. Which was insane yet would seem OK. She was as strong as an expert, yet every one of them are represented. Indeed how did the committee disregard somebody like her? Except if, did they think she was dead?

After everybody headed inside, I realized I expected to contact them, yet it was so hazardous with how strong that woman was. I could perhaps sneak it, ideally or I might be dead before I contact them.

I connected and figured out how to associate.

"We are in Colorado; I can't say all the more every one of the signs have been meddled with. There is a pack close by. Mo I can feel she took the Alpha's children you need to arrive quick. The pioneer is an expert of clairvoyance, its so undependable you have to arrive" I said overreacting I could essentially feel the peril coming towards me.

Chapter 11

I felt exceptionally uncovered even in

the shrubs. This was terrible so awful.

"Okay we will-" His voice was cut off. The blinding torment of a wrecked association made me unfit to think briefly. I believed I was being hauled and attempted to move yet the woman held me intellectually so I was unable to move.

She hauled me inside and down the steps then into a cell in a prison. I was drifting over the floor by her sorcery as she hauled me. Her face was terrifying with her glaring dreadfully. This was so terrible for me.

It was dim and sodden in here and smelled truly unpleasant.

Eww for what reason did she have a prison?

I attempted to arrive at anybody to say something. Crap poop poo crap. I was unable to utilize my powers. I truly trusted Mo will arrive soon before she kills me.

I saw composing on the wall. It was a name " Arlie Grather." That implies that Joan additionally tossed her in here as well, the unfortunate young lady.

I went through the backwoods driving the silly wolves to their demises. I halted in a clearing and paused. The wolves broke through the clearing and froze, I observed their ridiculous gags look round the field covered with

the assortments of their species. Like a tilde wave grasping washed over them yet before any of

them even attempted to go to hurry to caution every other person what they were going after. They fell down and died with a snap of my fingers and a bit of my powers streaming out of me. It was so natural, should taking lives be so natural?

I felt no regret, Joan had prepared that out of me along time prior. The whole field was loaded up with nothing living yet, myself. There was around twelve dead wolves now in this field. It taught them a lesson for attempting to whip us out. They were malevolent.

I grinned victoriously and cleaned the blood coming from the side of my eyes. That was the disadvantage of my powers. I began crying blood. It used to frighten the strict individuals when it occurred back when my powers were more erratic.

I was in Spain. The Violet pinnacle was around four blocks north, France had quite recently proclaimed battle on us. Well more explicitly the werewolf chamber who ran France had simply proclaim battle on us, the biggest otherworldly preparation tower in the world. I was around 100 years of age; I could move however had powers dim abnormal powers which made the committee exile me to the pinnacles. After a long evaluation of my capacities I was shipped off the Violet pinnacle. It was astonishing I felt acknowledged. Be that as it may, presently the werewolves were going to annihilate that, they were malevolent. I felt my wolf cry at that thought yet didn't differ since they constrained her out of her pack. I was strolling feeling the demise that was laid out underneath me. I was in an old church graveyard attempting to practice not having the dead stroll around me. It was very hard to keep them under control. I heard a shout and my eyes gobbled up to the cloister adherent remaining there shouting in fear at me. I didn't comprehend till I cleaned my eyes and saw blood. I overreacted and ran.

I shook my head to clear the memory, however it felt wrong.

The werewolf committee never went after the Violet pinnacle, they made the violet pinnacle. I wasn't 100 years of age; I was all things considered 50. I glanced around and saw that all the wolves didn't have blood on their gags, for what reason did I figure they did? I understood I was exceptionally near a wolf domain, that doesn't check out she said that as it were transitory conflict camps were around the pinnacle. This was an extremely durable, I felt so befuddled. I felt a sharp torment in my mind. The beast to me, my wolf, constraining a valid memory on me.

I was preparing at the Violet pinnacle; my powers had simply completely created, and I was being tried. The bloom in front of me gradually withered and passed on. I heaved I felt something wet on my hand and whipped it away it was blood. I turned upward and saw the analyzer was likewise dead. I

panted getting up. The entryway opened, I jumped to my feet forcing myself into the tight spot. I was unable to inhale, I had killed somebody.

"Please accept my apologies. I don't have any idea what occurred." I say overreacting,

another young lady came and assisted me with quieting down. She was decent and her power was to drop any remaining powers.

"It's OK you didn't have any idea what might occur, and neither did we. Come how about we go get you tidied up." The young lady said and I followed her.

I was confounded to the point that wasn't what I recollected however it felt right the other memory felt like it was constrained on to my mind. My head hurt so terrible I needed to plunk down. Yet I didn't let myself. Rather I returned to the red tower. My psyche was loaded up with questions. On the off chance that the werewolf committee made the pinnacles, why are they going after us? Is it true or not that they are going after us? When did I leave the violet pinnacle? What's more, Why?

I heard a whimper and realized it was my alpha kid. I felt the beast to me assume control over I was unexpectedly out of control as she ran, we didn't move. Stand by shift? I proved unable shift. She went through the backwoods to where he was laying.

He wasn't relaxing. I felt torment extreme agony like my world had finished. I let out a sound. I was unable to tell the beast separated from myself.

I inclined down petting his hair out of his face. He was so

attractive. I kissed his lips delicately, making my powers turn around his passing. I felt him return the kiss his hands going into my hair to hold me close. I pulled away to breath and looking at him dead without flinching. He expected to leave. I could never have him harmed again.

"I Arlie Grather reject you Alpha Hunter." I say he let out a cry and I ran off. I held up in the forest compelling the beast back behind the walls I worked, as I disregarded the crying, I could know about him. Then I returned to the tower. I was finished, a piece of me trusted that I would pass on the way back. I was unable to do this any longer regardless what Joan said.

I ought to feel unique, perhaps I am in shell shock. I heard individuals in fights get that. This was really the first time I was ever in the battle. I actually felt attracted to the alpha kid, that most likely implied that dismissal took a longer chance to set in.

I don't have the foggiest idea why I knew what to say for the dismissal, it felt more like the beast than me. The beast who was growling in my sub-conscience, her jaws needing to destroy who at any point had hurt him.

I had pushed the beast down somewhere down to me. Part of me felt it was anything but a beast. I strolled through the backwoods feeling like the woodland was calling me. Telling me to remain, letting me know only agony would come in the event that I kept

strolling. Perhaps returning to the boy wasn't past the point of no return.

Chapter 12

I could be blissful; I could feel how I could undoubtedly fall in love with him. Assuming I just barely let myself.

I could see our future to me. I would return he would take me to his pack. He would present me.

They could never know my past; it would be neglected for a delightful future together. We would get hitched.

He would check me; I would have his children. We would have two. A kid who closely resembles him somebody to take over the pack. Then a young lady, who was not at all like me. She didn't have risky abilities. I would neglect pretty much every one of the children that had kicked the bucket as a result of me.

I would

disregard their countenances; imagine I don't see them in my kids. Like I was certainly not a mass killer.

I shake my head. No, I can't do that. In the case of strolling back through the forest will just bring me torment and enduring, then, at that point, that is great. I merit it. I killed so many of them. Passing through the forest to the entryway. It was totally open; I keep thinking about whether they were all generally dead.

Other than it was past the point of no return, I dismissed him. That was conclusive.

Very much like what has been going on with my folks. I knew what happened now, I was furious. I pitched an attitude fit,

my powers came abruptly and killed them. Then I stood there shouting for them to awaken when my very strict babysitter came in and swooned from the blood dropping out of my eyes.

I was taken to the chamber who sent me to the violet tower. After that who knows and what difference does it make?

The house was in disorder when I got back. I saw a greater amount of our sort all over the place. In any case, they were not our troopers.

They were here to help definitely, how were there so many?

The turned when they saw me. I saw frightfulness on their faces, there was a gathering in lengthy shrouds. They were the committee; they were the ones who sent me away deserted me. Stand by no they didn't do that they sent me to the violet pinnacle they were simply attempting to help. I recoiled my head hurt so awful.

"Get on the ground!" one said. I gazed yet got down on my knees gradually the thing was occurring. I felt one come up behind me and bind me. I heaved I was unable to utilize my powers with these on I began to overreact. What is occurring?! I saw Joan, everything must be OK Joan would make sense of everything. She would fix this.

All that she did was correct, right?

"Joan, what's happening?" I asked dread in my voice everything was so unsure I was unable to help it. Actually she didn't answer, they constrained her to the ground. That wasn't

right, she should fix this.

"Joan Ofak, you will now be taken to jail for injustice and the utilization of your ability to control others for your own individual feud." One said I was so confounded. I saw bodies on the ground, it was my young ladies. They were all dead encompassed by dead wolves. Basically they went down with a battle, regardless of whether it was a battle that wasn't theirs.

I battled so hard attempting to draw near to her, however I couldn't move away from them. They were holding both of my arms. I saw Candice leave the house. How

did she arrive?

"You have utilized your clairvoyance powers to change others psyches and make them battle against wolves. Wolves who didn't have anything to do with your mate and your

little guy passing on." They said genuinely. I attempted to get to her overlooking what they said it can't be valid.

Candice ran in to the committee I heard what she was saying.

"That is Arlie she didn't have the foggiest idea what she was doing. I saw her brain Joan got her a wide range of screwed up. She ought to go to the silver pinnacle to assist with fixing her brain. She is super strong yet tossing her behind bars will simply support the possibility that you are against her." She said. Was she arguing my case? How could she do that? What was she discussing I understood what I was doing? Isn't that right?

I saw an Alpha and Luna come running. Two of the chamber individuals were holding small children. They put down the kids who went hurrying to the Alpha and Luna.

They were their children.

"Joan has been deceiving you. The wolves just went after since she took the Alphas kids. Also, the wolves are not beginning conflicts with us. They are making an effort not to end our species. Arlie we are wolves." Candice said. Indeed when did she get so close? I gazed at her. We are wolves?!

I was hauled away and placed into a strong vehicle like those that the human specialized squads use, and we drove away. I was distant from everyone else in the secondary lounge. Still fastened it was required, I

was a risk. Candice had gotten in the front seat. She continued to look back at me, she looked more seasoned. Indeed when did she grow up?

"Please accept my apologies. I work with the board. We heard things were going on oddly down here and came to research. I knew whether I told you, you might have a hard time believing me by any stretch of the imagination. This was the main way. The others… they are

gone. They kicked the bucket I'm heartbroken. We didn't make it in time."

She said delicately. I felt the words go through my cerebrum; I couldn't confide in anything any longer.

I peered out the back window I would rather not talk any longer or tune in. The red pinnacle was vanishing

behind us, my life vanishing behind us.

I actually look at myself in the mirror. My long fair hair was delicate looking and clean. My outfit was great with battle boots, dim tore thin pants, a white band shirt, and all polished off with my unmistakable calfskin coat. Thus, all things considered I was looking fucking hot.

I left my room and strolled deliberately towards the emergency clinic region of the pinnacle. I actually wasn't assumed to do this. I was after all an organizer for exploring missions, yet hello I checked out the young lady. She was brought into the world in France as was I. We had an association, even however I had never seen her in my life. After much digging, we had found who she truly was and how Joan had viewed as her. Joan had taken the unfortunate young lady in the late evening from the Violet pinnacle. There were a few horrendous recollections about a conflict from the werewolf committee in France going after and individuals biting the dust all over her. At the point when truly it was really a festival with firecrackers, not a conflict. Joan was areas of strength for insanely, sadly she must be eliminated of her powers. A awful business however she is excessively perilous and excessively far gone to save.

What occurred with her was she had a mate and kid.

In any case, a rouge broke into her home and killed her mate also, kid. She then like all wolves went crazy.

Chapter 13

How no one saw or realized they were dead is mind boggling, in like a terrible way. She then, at that point, framed a feud against all wolves, including her own wolf which she pushed in the back of her brain. Then Joan went the Violet pinnacle and gotten to know a youthful receptive young lady. Following a month of chipping away at her she took her.

Indeed, the clumsiness of our sort is absurd.

Since nobody saw and when they did, they accepted the unfortunate young lady just ran off. Imbeciles the parcel of them.

The closure of that insane battle had been seven days prior. The princeps was currently remaining in the silver pinnacle, the best tower however I might be a piece one-sided since I have lived here my whole life. She was in the psychological medical clinic segment however on the grounds that well, her psyche was screwed up from Joan.

I thumped on her emergency clinic entryway and didn't hear her hollering so concluded that implied I would simply stroll in. Her hair was a touch longer. She was in certain scours sitting on the floor. Her room was great yet exceptionally unoriginal I given careful consideration to fix that. She wanted some tone in here.

I wasn't stressed over her killing me or anything with

those insane great powers of hers. Since one her room was warded to dissipate all deadly utilization of abilities. Furthermore, since I am so astounding, and a conjurer, I captivated my calfskin coat with assurance spells against basically everything. Meaning I would be impeccably safe; other than I was there to get to know her. The excess living individuals from her pack were shipped off different pinnacles. Well aside from Cassandra, however well she had learned it was her who double-crossed them, so we found it best not to have Cassandra around her by any means.

"Hi I am Morpheus. What's your name delightful?" I asked sitting on the floor with her. She gave me a odd look; I wasn't her primary care physician she knew that. I was taking a stab at something to check whether she would get it or not.

"Ariel." She said, I realized that was off-base. Her genuine name was Lissette, however like I said her psyche was screwed up. The insane woman Joan had totally changed her character, which I had perused people do while shaping a faction, so it appears to be legit. Joan made her totally dependent on anything that she said.

"Sweet. Well this is for you." I say giving her a new hairbrush that had fasteners folded over it. She looked a touch befuddled and took it.

"Much appreciated?" She said and I grinned and left. In this way, she didn't understand that we were talking in French. Fascinating, I gave her the hairbrush since she didn't have one.

I searched in the little window to her room and saw her grinning delicately brushing her hair. I clench hand knock then, at that point, saw the head mind healer and ran so she didn't understand who was wrongfully in the medical clinic segment. I anticipated visiting again tomorrow, this would be the beginning of a awesome fellowship!

Thanks for reading

THE END

www.ingramcontent.com/pod-product-compliance
Lightning Source LLC
LaVergne TN
LVHW080818170826
845678LV00011B/2066
* 9 7 9 8 8 3 7 2 7 9 2 7 0 *